Mark's Cars

Mark lost one of his cars again.
He asked his dad for help.

"Dad, do you have my black car?" Mark asked. "It's not large."

"I don't have the car. I saw it when we got back from the marshes at the park," said Dad. "The car can't be far, so think hard, Mark!"

"Hmm," Mark said. "It can't be far!"

Mark put his arm under his bed. It was hard to see because it was dark. He does see a sock and a block.

"No car so far," said Mark.

Mark looked in his boxes.

"I think I saw my car in here," said Mark as he started to take every part of the boxes apart.

"It's not here," he said.

Mark looked in every place.

"It can't be far," said Mark, "because Dad said he saw the car when we came back from the park."

He started over again.

"I can't find my car," Mark said as he waved his arms. "And I've started a mess."

Just then, Mark looked at his art set and saw an odd shape in the jar of brushes.

"It's my black car!" said Mark. "I forgot that when we got back from the park, I used my car to spark my art!"

Phonics Fun

Write a word you know that will help you remember words with r-controlled ar.

Comprehension

Would you tell a friend to read this book? Why?

Decodable Words

apart	large
arm	Mark
art	marsh
car	park
dark	part
far	spark
hard	start
jar	

High Frequency Words

again	does
because	every

15